Jenny Oldfield

my little life

When Scott Got Lost

illustrated by Martina Farrow

Hodder Children's Books

a division of Hodder Headline Limited

First published in Great Britain in 2002
by Hodder Children's Books

10 9 8 7 6 5 4 3 2 1

All characters in this publication are fictitious and any resemblance to real persons, living or dead, is purely coincidental.

A Catalogue record for this book is available from the British Library

ISBN 0 340 85073 6

Printed and bound in Great Britain by
Bookmarque Ltd, Croydon, Surrey

Hodder Children's Books
A division of Hodder Headline Limited
338 Euston Road, London NW1 3BH

A big thank you to the hundreds of kids I met on school visits who helped me with ideas for these books!

Sunday, October 13th

***Your stars** – A family gathering is coming up. Instead of throwing a strop, make an effort with the relleys and have fun the way only Leos can.*

Wrong, wrong, WRONG!
My family isn't gathering, it's falling apart at the seams.

Shah's horoscope says she's bursting with bright ideas. She has to get busy decorating her bedroom. I texted her to pick-up-a-paint-brush and go-mad-with-murals. She texted me back: 'Tiff, What u on abt? Pakng 4 tmorrow. Hw mny prs shorts u tking?'

I texted back and told her two, which is all I have.

Geri's stars put her on a choccy overdose alert (no kidding).

My text message to her – 'Lve out choccy biccies!'

Geri's to me – '2 late. Am alrdy pakd, inc. 15 KitKats.'

Ellie's stars promise, 'You'll find mega bargains on a shopping spree.'

Decided not to text her. She doesn't need ME to tell her to go out and spend, spend, spend!

When we sat and made our lists of stuff to take on this trip, and we put Ellie's and mine side by side, this is how they looked:

Ellie	Tiffany
orange Goretex	Mum's blue cagoule
black leather jacket	denim jacket
blue jeans x 3	jeans x 2
black trousers x 2	shorts x 2
shorts x 3 (1 blue, 2 black)	T-shirts x 4
walking boots	trainers
short-sleeved tops x 6	sweatshirts x 2
long-sleeved tops x 6	socks x 4
evening tops x 4	wellies
trainers	undies x 6
socks x 8 (2 spare)	bra
undies x 8	nightie
bras x 4	swimmie
nighties x 3	torch
swimmies x 2 (+1 bikini)	
etc. . .	

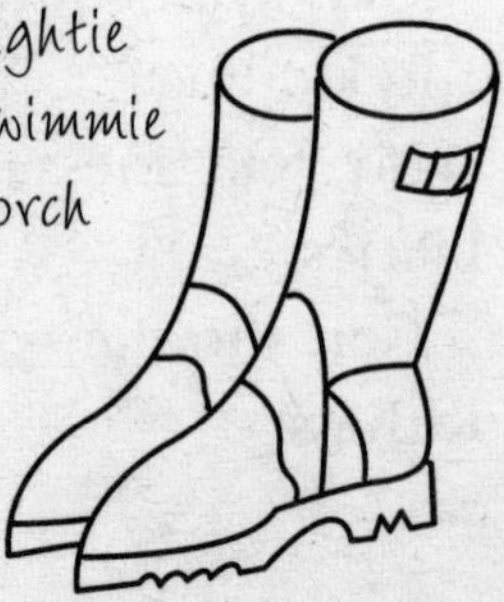

Ellie's went on twice as long. Make-up, minidisc player, Armani perfume. Her bag will weigh a ton. Good job it's got wheels.

I am so looking forward to our trip – NOT!

Other schools get to go skiing in the Alps, or paragliding in Greece. Not Ashbrook kids. What do we get? A week in the wet, a lurk by the lake. Five days at Frizinghall (Freezinghole). Shiver-drip gasp-grumble!

Scott's been before, when he was in Year 7. He's going again this year, on a training programme for when he flies to Patagonia next summer, after GCSEs. That's him, Nic (Hunk) Heron and Marc (Music Man) Ainsworth (from

Year 9). They were specially selected to join a Northern Schools Explorers Scheme. So the three boys get a second sesh at Frizinghall as part of their training, then they jet off to South America, as long as they raise the money themselves and do the training. That's a laugh – my slob brother never raises so much as an arm if he can help it!

And my falling-apart family doesn't have any dosh to give him. Dad owes Mum for half the house and Mum's spending everything she earns on furniture and stuff for her new flat. So poor old Scott looks like being penniless in Patagonia, abandoned in the Andes.

In English on Friday, Mr Fox taught us alliteration. 'Tell Tiffany to try teaching Tom to tango'. 'Ellie evidently excels in expenditure'. 'Slovenly Scott slouches slobbishly on the sofa'.

I went round for hours alliterating everything in sight, until Geri yelled at me to stop.

'I'm practising poetic patterns,' I told her. Puh-puh-puh.

'Get lost, Tiffany!'

'What's wrong? You practise your overhead

smash, and do I complain? No way. I just sit and watch without a squeak!'

'Tennis is different.'

'Tisn't.'

'Tis!' Geri bounces around the place like a ball. Bounce, smash, bam! Tennis rules OK. Poetry is pants.

She scrawled 'Tiffany Talks Trash!' on my pencil case. It doesn't put me off being a famous writer one day, but it sure teaches me when to keep quiet.

4.30pm – Had a massive row with Scott. He came into my room and grabbed the one and only rucksack. I'd already packed my nightie, my swimmie and my knickers in it. He shook the bag upside down and emptied everything on to the floor. I lost it completely. In between scrabbling for the knickers (mega embarrassing), I was yelling and screaming blue murder.

'I found it first!'

'It's my rucksack, ratface!'

'Tisn't!' Tug, wrench, wrestle to get it back. 'Snot fair! Dad, help! Ouch! Scott's twisting my arm, he's hurting me!'

Dad poked his head around the door. 'Scott, put your sister down,' he said calmly.

'Not until she lets me have the rucksack!' Scott didn't know it, but he'd got one of my pairs of knickers hooked on to his foot. White, with Bart Simpson on the front.

'Tiffany, let Scott have the rucksack.' Dad took one look and cracked out laughing.

'It's not his. It was in the attic. I found it first!' I was going in for Round 2, headbutting Scott in the stomach.

'Yeah, but I'm the one who has to camp out in the freezing cold, while you Year 7s stay in the nice warm hall. I need this to carry my tent and sleeping bag.' Long speech from normally silent big bro. Then he saw Bart staring up at him and shook his foot like a shark had grabbed it.

'Yeah, it looks like Scott's right,' Dad chuckled. 'Tiff, give him the bag. You can take my Adidas hold-all.'

I let go of Scott and the rucksack. Wow, thanks Dad! His bag goes back to the olden days, when he played footie for his local team. It's all grungy and smelly. So I went into a major strop, grabbed my phone and called Mum to borrow a bag from her.

Neil answered. How bad can a day get?

Neil: Hello.
Me: Neil?
Neil: Yeah, who's that?
Me: It's me, Tiffany. Is Mum there?
Neil: Hi, Tiff. Yeah, hold on a sec.

Smoothie, smarmy Neil. I've only met him once and he calls me Tiff.

He came back to the phone. 'Actually, Tiff, Gina's in the shower right now. Can I get her to call you back?'

Me: No, it's OK, it's not important.
Neil: Can I pass on a message?
Me: No thanks. Say I'll ring her when I get back from my school trip.

I clicked off the phone fast.

Dad rubbed his forehead as if he had a bad headache. 'Did your mum give you any extra pocket money for the trip?' he asked.

Without waiting for an answer, he dug in his pocket and came out with a few scruffy notes. He handed over twenty quid.

I could've cried. I tried to hand it back, saying there was nothing to spend it on where I was going. Freezing Hole is in the middle of nowhere. There are no shops or anything.

Course, Scott comes in with, 'No problem, I'll take it!' pretending to snatch the money out of my hand.

I flicked Bart at his face and he soon backed off.

Dad will be on his own next week, except for Bad-Breath Bud.

Monday, October 14th

Your Stars *– Feeling dull? Add sparkle to your life with a new accessory such as glitter stars for your nails.*

Yeah, like decorating my fingernails is gonna solve all my problems!

Chaos on bus alert! Shah left her bag in her dad's car boot and ended up with no changes of clothes. She'll have to wear the same thing for the whole week. Chucky and Squealer threatened to throw up on the back seat – 'Sir, sir, I had kippers for breakfast. I think I'm gonna puke!' And the driver took a wrong turning at Forde Abbey, so we ended up going back the way we'd just come.

'Brilliant start!' Ellie said. Sarcasm is her latest thing.

'Take me home!' I groaned. I was sitting in the direct firing line of Chucky and Squealer.

'Don't be a wimp,' Geri told me. She's the weird type who looks forward to climbing mountains and going white water rafting. The danger of people puking over her is nothing to make a fuss about either.

Fuchsia quickly changed the subject. 'Ellie, can I borrow a sweatshirt and some trousers?'

Ellie talked designer labels and decided which of her five pairs she could bear to part with.

'The wheels on the bus go round and round,
Round and round, round and round . . .'

Chucky, Squealer and Callum croaked from the back seat as the driver got stuck trying to turn

around in a narrow lane. Black and white cows poked their heads over the hedge and mooed.

> *'The people on the bus go honk-honk-honk,*
> *Honk-honk-honk, honk-honk-honk!'*

They mimed puking up their guts then fell about laughing. That's their typical caveman humour. Ugh-ugh! Miss Hornby put a stop to it by handing out our detailed program of activities. Orienteering, caving, rowing, rock-climbing . . . That's when I started to feel seriously sick myself. CAVING . . . ROCK CLIMBING!!!

'How about the Calvin Kleins?' Ellie asked Shah.

'Miss, can I put my name down for caving?' Geri was first in line, natch.

'I wanna go home!' I groaned.

'Shut up, Tiff, and write your diary!' Geri snapped. 'If you're gonna be a pain, do it quietly!'

Bad news – the driver found his way.

More bad news – I'm not sharing a dorm with any of my best mates. How did that happen?

Even more bad news – it's peeing down.

The worst news – tomorrow morning I have to go caving. Underground. In the dark. Nightmare!

There's no good news that I can think of right now.

'The house was miles from anywhere. It stood among trees in what had once been a garden, looking as if it had been there since the beginning of time.'

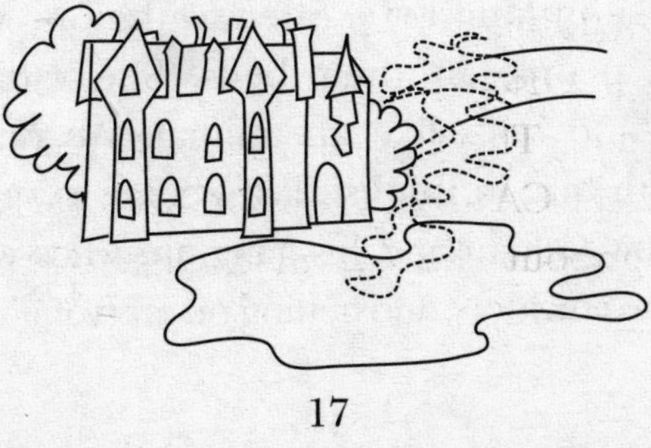

I can use Frizinghall in my ghost story. Must make notes.

Moss on roof, crooked chimneys, built of stone. Arched stone doorway and windows. Looks out over lake. Windy, rainy. Mist rolling in over the moor. Spooky!

My story house is haunted, I know that much. There's a body sealed up inside a thick wall – just bones and a blood-stained knife. One of the characters discovers the skeleton and gets possessed by the ghost.

> 'The voice of the ghost hissed through the trees. There was no escape. It cried through the walls of its hidden tomb, "My blood will cry out in generations to come. It will seek vengeance, and curse this house forever!"'

When we first got here, Mr Fox took one look and said there was probably a mad woman in the attic, like in Jane Eyre. She was the one who set fire to people in their beds. She rattles her chains and bites like an animal. We read that part with him in English last week.

So now Callum and his gang are whoo-whooing down the corridors, and getting on everyone's nerves.

I said to Shah, 'What did we do to deserve this?' But at least it's not so bad for her, she's in a dorm with Ellie and Geri.

'Ask to swap rooms,' she told me. 'Or, better still, I'll get Claire to swap with you, no sweat.'

Claire gets on with Mel and Laura, who are in my room, so it makes sense. Shah's like that – she thinks about other people.

Resolution: TRY TO BE A NICE PERSON!!

Methods: Help Geri to be a tennis superstar
Stop feeling jealous of Ellie
Be more like Shah
Stop moaning about stuff I don't want to do
Be nice to Scott (mega hard)

Have moved rooms, thanks to Shah.

Am in strange, hard bed with proper sheets and blankets.

Am using torch to write diary while others are asleep. A tree outside is so close it rattles

against the window pane. I've heard an owl, seen a bat and

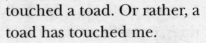

touched a toad. Or rather, a toad has touched me.

It was down by the lake when we were learning how to use our life-jackets. Pull this, press that, set off a flare and hopefully float. Squealer spotted the toad squatting on a rock and poked it with a stick. The poor thing croaked, hopped and landed splat on my wellie. It was BIG! And GROSS!

'Wicked!' Chucky chortled.

'Uerrkk! Errrrkkkk!' The toad looked like it had had the shock of its life. It was browny-grey, slimy and covered in lumps.

I totally lost it. 'Get it off me! Yuck! Uggh! Uerrrk!'

Miss Hornby gave me the evil eye and tugged another toggle. Her life-jacket hissed and bulged.

I raised my wellie and shook my foot. The toad clung on. 'Use your stick, poke it again!' I screeched at Adam (Adam Pigg = Squealer. Ha ha). 'Go on, poke it!'

Let's face it, I'll never make President of the World Wildlife Fund.

Before anything horrible could happen to the

toad, Shah stepped in and picked it up. WITH BARE HANDS! She cupped it between her palms and tickled its head with her finger.

'Uerrk! Uerrk!' It seemed to like it.

'Errgh, look it's puffing out its throat!' I groaned.

'No jokes about kissing it, puh-lease!' Geri begged the boys.

'Cool – it looks like Miss Hornby in her life-jacket!' Ellie giggled. 'Anyhow, it couldn't possibly be uglier than some boys in our class I could mention!'

'Fuchsia, put down that toad and pay attention!' Miss Hornby likes Ellie and Geri, but not me and Shah. She says we mess about too much and waste time. I have to admit that Games is not my best subject.

Had supper in ginormous, long room with a shield and crossed swords above the fireplace. There's a dead deer on the wall, with huge antlers and glass eyes. I s'pose you have to take out the brain and stuff the head with straw or something. The eyes look like they're following you around the room.

After, we moved to the Games room – ping-pong and table-football. A good laugh. Girls won the football, 12–9. Then Heather and Gorgeous George came out of the corner where they'd been having a 'serious conversation' and suggested a sing-song. Well, as lead singer of the school band, Ellie was up like a flash.

'C'mon, Marc, c'mon, Dom!' She pushed Dom towards a tatty old, out-of-tune piano. The three of them make up half of Gemini, Heather's pet Drama and Music Department project.

'Who else can sing?' Mr Fox asked, looking straight at me. I shook my head. I'd rather die. 'Fuchsia can!' I piped up. Big foot in mouth time.

So Shah got hauled up by Ellie, which is weird when you think back to the fact that Ellie sneakily 'used' Shah's voice to get into the band in the first place. Anyhow, there they were, butter-wouldn't-melt, and Dom was starting to tootle a tune and we all sat back and enjoyed the show.

Ellie danced – I wannabe a popstar, I wanna

make a video, I wannabe f-a-m-o-u-s! She was mega-tastic.

Shah was up there too. They go well together – Ellie all blonde hair and sparkly white teeth, Shah with dark curly hair and amazing big brown eyes. I reckon they were cool – easily good enough to make it if they want to.

'Who's that other one?' Scott's friend, Nic Heron, had dragged himself away from table football to watch and listen. Year 11s never notice us, so this was a big thing.

'You mean, not Ellie?' I stammered. Hammering heart, a frog in my throat. I mean, Nic Heron! 'That's Fuchsia Allerton. She's in my tutor group.'

I could see him thinking, Hmm, she's a babe.

What can I say?

THE BIG TEST OF BEING A NICE PERSON: Shall I tell Shah that Nic fancies her and wreck any chance I ever had of getting him to look at me as anything else except Scott's kid sister?

Reasons to fancy Nic:
- Super cool guy
- Brilliant skateboarder
- Not bigheaded
- Not a slob

Reasons for him not to notice me:
- 4 years younger
- ears too big
- not super cool
- can't skateboard

In fact, not a snowball in Hades chance, as my dad would say.

So I might as well tell Shah – maybe tomorrow.

Torch is beginning to fade. Must buy new battery from post office in village.

Hopes fade, the beam dies
The flickering flashlight
Illumines dark lies
In the still heart of night.

(Flashlight = metaphor for truth, searching out the way we fool ourselves when we fancy someone.) I mean, Nic Heron luvs Tiffany Little. Who am I kidding? Nic = School soccer-playing, skateboarding hunk. Tiffany = scraggy no-hoper about to smack headlong into puberty. I only bought my first training bra because I was the last in my Games group to have one, not because it actually has anything to train.

'On average, girls in the year 2001 reach puberty 2 years earlier than their grandmothers did.' It's official. I read it in a problem page. *'Dear Ceri, I'm ten years old and embarrassed by the size of my boobs (size 34C). What shall I do?' 'Dear Alyssa, Don't worry, you are not alone. On average, girls in the year 2001 blah-blah . . .'*

I'm a throwback to 1950, a misfit, a freak.

Tuesday, October 15th

***Your stars** – Rain is boring so why not make an indoor treasure hunt for a friend? You'll soon forget about the lousy weather!*

Who do they write these things for? Why do I

keep on reading them? Answer in not more than 50 words to tiffany.little@hodder.co.uk.

Today, I get to go caving. Of which, more later – *if* I survive!

OK, Caving is the pits! It stinks. No human being should ever consider doing it. I mean, squirming down a crack in the rock, wriggling through a wet tunnel, coming out into a cave with stalactitey things hanging from the ceiling then plunging through a waterfall on to a ledge just wide enough to take one person wearing a white plastic crash helmet and a soaked cagoule.

Nightmare, or what?

George took digital pictures of each of us bursting through the wall of water. He got them up on screen this lunchtime. Geri's launching herself on to the ledge like she was born to be a caver.

She's punching through the water like Lara Croft. Ellie's kind of elegantly striding through in her orange Goretex, making a fashion statement with the angle of her crash hat. Shah's frowning as if she's concentrating really hard. And me? Think drowned rat, think non-waterproof cagoule and sticky-out ears. Mr Fox showed me the picture and I zapped the Delete button before anyone else could see.

'"Four Go Caving!"' he grinned. 'Maybe Enid Blyton was on to something after all!'

We were drying out beside the big fire in the dining hall when Scott showed up. Well, Scott, Nic and Marc, actually. They're the ones doing the serious training for next year, and no way does Scott let you forget it.

'I'm *beep-beeping* knackered!' he groaned, barging in on our cosy, steaming circle. He flung his gloves and hat on to the hearth and made room for himself on the sofa. Scott doesn't sit, he splurges. Nic perched on one arm and Marc on the other.

'We've been fell racing,' Marc explained.

'Sounds painful,' Ellie got in before we had time to move our steamy butts. We'd all been standing with our backs to the fire, recovering from the waterfall.

'Five *beeping* miles!' My brother's manners suck. His feet were already up on the coffee table and he was hogging the fire. 'It was *beeping* down and the *beep-beeping* wind knocked us off our *beeping* feet. We could've died of hypo-*beeping*-thermia!'

'Ignore him,' I told the others. 'Scott and exercise don't mix.'

'Yeah well, how come I got chosen by the Northern Schools Expedition Society?'

'I expect they were desperate.'

Scott picked up a wet sock and flung it at me.

'So how was your morning?' Nic asked Fuchsia.

'Cool,' Geri broke in. 'We saw this mega limestone cave with a waterfall!' She didn't even notice that she'd interrupted. 'Miss Hornby says it's got some of the longest stalactites in the country!'

'Huh, stalac-*beeping*-tites!' Mutter from Scott, who was excavating dirt from behind his fingernails and flicking it towards the fire.

I gave him a glare.

'What're you doing this afternoon?' Nic asked Shah.

'Rowing on the lake!' Geri gushed.

Ellie raised her eyebrows at me. 'C'mon, Tiff, let's go.'

Gladly. I flounced after her in my wet jeans, hearing Nic tell Shah that it was orienteering for them, and Geri breaking in again, bash-bam-zap!

'What's orienteering?' Ellie asked me.

'Y'know, learning how to read a compass and use a map. Very useful when you're in Outer Patagonia, I guess.'

Ellie led the way to the dining room. 'How come they don't just take a guide?'

I shrugged. 'This is in case they get lost. Knowing Scott's lousy sense of direction, that wouldn't be hard, believe me!'

My Mastermind big bro says left when he means right. Mum and Dad lost count of the times they had to go and pick him up from the Lost Children's tent on Blackpool beach.

'Go on, Tiff, write us a song!' Ellie shouted across the Games room.

We'd rowed and sloshed around all afternoon on a grey lake, got our oars tangled in slimy weeds, then vanished in a thick white mist

that swept down from Three Cols. 'Don't panic!' Miss Hornby blew her whistle from the shore and we all rowed, panicking like mad, towards the sound.

'I'm too young to die!' drama-queen Ellie shrieked. She was in a boat with Geri. Soon a flare shot up through the fog.

'Ellie Shelbourn, for goodness sake, stop messing around!' Miss Hornby's voice went squeaky. 'Just keep on rowing and stay calm.'

Finally we all made it to the shore. The mist disappeared and we stood on the pebbles feeling stupid while Miss H phoned the Mountain Rescue team to say not to worry, that the distress flare had been set off by mistake.

'Well, I don't care what people say!' Ellie said, holding her head high. 'If that wasn't an emergency, I don't know what is!'

I was glad when supper came, then we dashed to grab the ping-pong bats in the Games room, and – oh no! – Ellie suggested I should write a Number One hit single for Gemini!

(Food great, by the way. Fat chips with everything.)

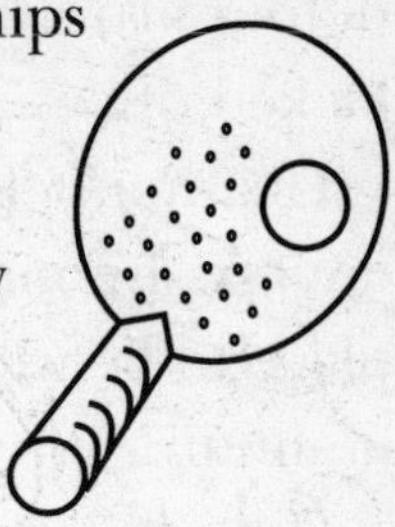

'Ssshhh!' I hissed at Ell.

Geri served the skiddly-diddly ball at me and sent it whizzing past my backhand side. 'Eight-love!' she cried.

'C'mon, Tiff, don't be a wimp. Everyone knows you're good at poetry and stuff. You write the lyrics and get Shah to do the music!' Ellie was really into it.

'Nine-love!' Another 90 mph serve flashed by me.

I fished the ball out from under the table-football stand.

'Hey, what's this I hear?' Heather swept in to save me from mega defeat. She took the bat and ball, then whisked me away from the ping-pong to have a serious talk. 'George has already mentioned to me that you write well. So, really, what about creating original words and have Shah work on the music?'

I shrugged and stared at a spider crawling across the floor. 'I'm busy writing a ghost story.'

'That's great. Does George know?'

I shook my head. The spider did a quick

detour around a dead trainer that someone had kicked off.

Heather's the type of teacher who's so full of energy she makes you feel tired. 'This is a great place to be writing a spooky horror story. What's it about?'

'Two brothers. One murders the other and hides the body inside a thick stone wall. It all happens ages ago, and the house is cursed. The dead brother haunts it.' It sounded stupid when I told her.

'Great idea. You could call it *Blood Brothers*, only I'm afraid someone already thought of it.' Chit-chatting away, she eventually brought me back round to the song for Gemini. To cut a long story short, I agreed to do it.

'But only if you write the music,' I whispered to Shah when everyone else had gone off to bed.

'Listen, I still haven't let you off for making me stand up in front of everyone and sing with Ellie last night!' Shah pointed out.

'Oh yeah, sorry about that.'

'Honest, Tiff, you need to work on your self-image.' Shah gets this style of talk from her mum and dad. They're happy hippies. 'You should enjoy the fact that you're good with words.'

'Doesn't it make me look like a geek?'

'No way.'

'Sure?'

'Listen, Michelle Clarke is a geek. So is Andrew Ribston. You are *not*, OK!'

I nodded. Compared with those two super-brains I was pretty normal, even I could see that.

'Anyway, how about you?' I argued back. 'You're the best singer in the school, yet you didn't even audition for Gemini!'

Shah went bright red. 'OK, so we're both wimps!'

'So do we wanna write a song?' I asked.

There was a long pause. A song for Ellie. I'd probably call it 'Look at Me!' and it would go something like this:

'*Look at me*
Can't you see
It's meant to be
Look look look at me!'

(Am failing big time to be a nice person, I realize.)

Shah wrinkled her nose like a rabbit, then filled the silence. 'Nah!' she said. 'We don't wanna do that!'

We let ourselves off the hook.

'Y'know what,' I confided. 'Nic Heron fancies you.'

Shah pulled more rabbit faces. 'No way!'

'He does. He asked me who you were.'

'So?'

'So, that means he fancies you!'

'Leave it out, Tiff!'

'Why? You should be flattered.' There's a rule in our year that when an older kid notices you, it doesn't matter what he looks like, it's still a buzz. And Nic's a drop-dead gorgeous hunk.

'Yeah, but y'know what'll happen if Ellie and the others find out. It'll be all round the school that Nic's a cradle snatcher and next time I see him, he'll cut me dead.'

I nodded. Shah was probably right.

'Anyhow, even if it's true, I know you won't spread it.' She leaned forward and poked at the remains of the log fire. Sparks flew up the chimney. 'Like you didn't breathe a word about Skye.'

This is Shah's BIG SECRET.

'I wouldn't,' I told her. 'I didn't even write it down in my diary.'

She thought for a long time. 'I would't mind if

you did. No one reads your diary, do they?'

'They die if they do!'

She managed to grin. 'So, you can mention it then.' Even so, I feel weird. This is it: the bare facts. Skye is Fuchsia's half-sister. She's sixteen and lives in Scotland. Shah and her mum only just found out about her, and it was by accident. Shah's dad had to eat dirt and admit that he had a secret older daughter. Wow, imagine! It's a mega problem for the whole family, especially since Skye now wants to come down and meet her dad. I feel sorry for Shah, I really do.

Wednesday, October 16th

***Your stars** – You're over-excited at the moment, so take some time to chill out.*

Scott's is:

– Make sure you help out at home during the next month. Someone's gonna have a mega strop if they see you slumped in front of the TV once too often.

. . . not really. I made that up. This morning Scott has to set off up the Three Cols with Nic and Marc. They have to camp on the mountain and cook their own food, sleep two nights, then find their way back down. The weather forecast says rain.

I was feeling sorry for him until breakfast. Then we had meltdown.

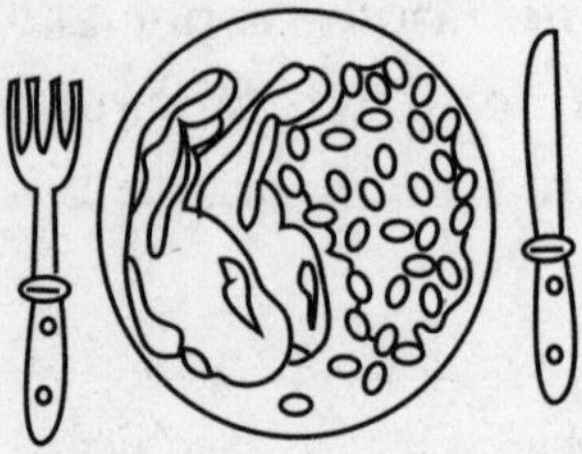

It was like this. I'm tucking into bacon and beans, looking forward to white water rafting – NOT. Kids are banging and crashing about with plates and cutlery, dashing to fetch an extra layer of clothes, or just dossing. In other words, the dining room is chocka-block full.

In rushes Marc Ainsworth waving something white and lacy. 'Scott Little wears girls' pants!' he croaks. 'Look what I just found in his rucksack!'

Oh God! I recognise those rosebuddy knickers (present from Gran Jackson)! They must've got stuck in the bottom of the rucksack when Scott and I had that row.

Scott charges after Marc and makes a grab for the pants. Everyone is falling around laughing, and I'm crawling under the table. Let's face it, me and underwear have a nightmare relationship.

'Give 'em 'ere, you *beeper*!' Scott lunges at Marc and grabs the knickers. Marc holds on. They rip.

Mr Fox comes in and separates Scott and Marc. 'Just grow up, you two!' He takes the shredded knickers from them, looks at me and realizes they must be mine. So does everyone else in the room. Mr F throws them in the bin and walks out.

My stomach has churned into knots and I find it hard to swallow. I push the rest of my breakfast away and disappear fast. Ellie follows, full of sympathy for once.

'Never mind, Tiff. We all know what an idiot Marc is. Do you want me to tell you a secret about him, that I heard from Squealer?'

'No.' I shake my head. 'Let me just crawl away and die!'

10.00 hours. I s'pose Scott, Marc and Nic have already set off for the mountains, and I hope they freeze to death, except Nic of course.

I'm hiding in the Games room from Miss Hornby, hoping that she won't notice I'm missing from Group B. Group A, including Geri, is already rafting like crazy through the white water that runs into the lake. It's pouring down like they said.

This morning, Squealer left the shower on and flooded his dorm, so he's stayed behind to clear it all up. Chucky Gilbert twisted his ankle coming downstairs, clumsy idiot. He might get sent home early because of it. Hmm, now there's an idea . . .

Spent a while studying my reflection in the long mirror in the girls' cloakroom. The left side of my face looks better than the right. My nose on that side is a nicer shape. Hair's not bad this length (nearly to my shoulders). But the things I can't do anything about are my naff ears. Will just have to wear my hair long to cover them for the rest of my entire life.

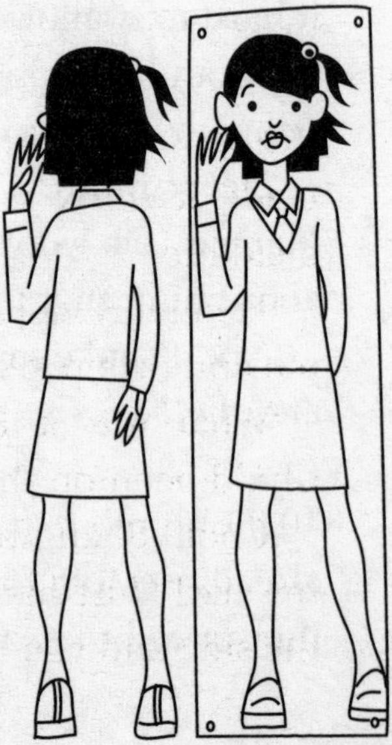

Read this fact in a mag – the only part of your anatomy that keeps on growing when you get old is your – wait for it – ears. Aaagh!

When I'm sixty, I'm gonna look like an elephant.

13.00 hours. At 10.30 Geri came looking for me. She said Miss H was having a major strop. 'Honest, Tiff, she says if you don't show up in the next five minutes, you can kiss goodbye to a decent end-of-term report!'

Hornby is our group tutor, so you have to keep in with her. My theory is that only power-mad types get to be Games teachers. They like to make you suffer.

I sighed a lot, then told Geri to let her know I'd be there. I grabbed my cagoule and finally made it thirty seconds inside the five minute deadline.

'Helmet. Life-jacket.' Hornby shoved them at me and ordered me to stand in line.

'What was it like?' Ellie was asking Shah, who'd been on the raft with Geri.

'Cool.' Shah was shivering from head to foot, the liar! 'Just hang on to the rope attached to the side and you'll be OK.'

'Remember, keep these life-jackets on at all times!' Hornby instructed her next group of helpless victims. 'This is a tough activity, so I don't want anyone messing around.'

I swear she frowned right at me and Shah. We were standing under some tall pine trees, catching the drips. The stream roared and gushed at our feet.

'Don't you get a buzz, just looking at it!' Geri sighed.

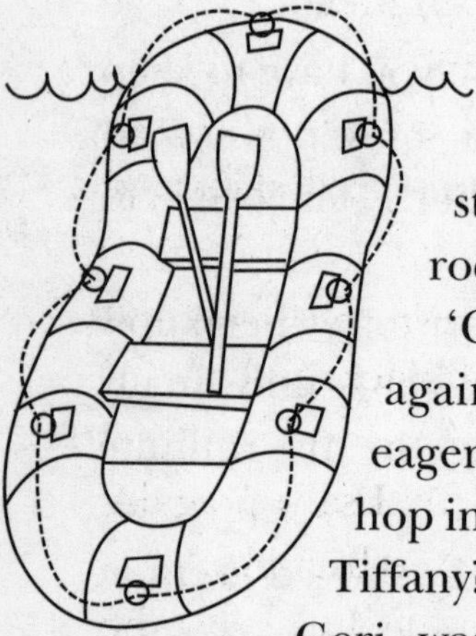

'No!' I was concentrating on the raft – a black rubber inflatable thing with yellow stripes. What if it hit a sharp rock and burst?

'Geri, you look keen to go again.' Miss H picked up her eager-beaver expression. 'Why not hop into this next raft with Ellie and Tiffany? Show them how it's done.'

Geri was in like a flash. 'Grab a paddle!' she yelled at Ellie, keeping the other one for herself. 'Tiff, you just sit in the middle and hold the thing steady, OK!'

NOT OK, but what difference did it make? We were off.

The current took hold and swept us into the white water. Cold spray blew in my face as I crouched in the middle and let Ellie and Geri paddle.

We bobbed and whirled, rocked and rolled between two huge boulders. Ellie's paddle scraped the bank and almost snapped.

'Isn't this cool!' Geri yelled above the roar of the water.

We tilted and tipped, water leaked in, Ellie screamed and I closed my eyes tight shut.

'Lean to the right!' Geri cried.

I forced my eyes open to see a gigantic cliff in front of us. We leaned sideways and skimmed around a sharp bend.

'Ouch!' I was thrown forwards on to my left shoulder and got a face full of black rubber.

'Tiff, look out!'

This time Geri was too late. As I sat up again, my helmet went smack into a tree branch.

My whole life passed before me and I saw the headline:

SCHOOLGIRL DECAPITATED BY PINE TREE!

But luckily we swept on and my head was still attached to my shoulders.

'Only three more minutes before we reach the end!' Geri promised. 'Just sit tight, Tiff, you'll be fine!'

'Miss, she hit her head!' Ellie explained to Miss Hornby how come I was staggering on the shore.

I'd sat tight like Geri said and spent the next three minutes making a plan. Like no way, NO WAY was I gonna do anything like this ever again!

'Let me take a look,' Hornby said. Geri had run upstream to fetch her when she saw me stagger out of the raft.

Before the teacher reached me, I collapsed in a heap.

'Miss, what's wrong with her?' Ellie whimpered.

H tried to lean me up against a rock, but I groaned. She let me lie there instead.

'Is she unconscious?' I heard Ellie losing it. 'Has she broken something? Miss, shall we set off a flare?'

'Not yet! Stand back, let me think.'

For Ellie's sake, I thought I'd best open my eyes. In another second she would be getting out her mobile and calling the Rescue helicopter. So I flickered my lids and turned my head.

'Tiff, are you all right?' There were real tears in Ellie's eyes.

I moaned and pointed feebly to my left shoulder.

'Miss, she fell on it!' Ellie gasped.

'Hmm. Tiffany, can you move your left arm?'

I tried and yelped.

'Can you wiggle your fingers?'

I nodded and wiggled.

'But you can't lift the arm? How about trying to sit up?'

I managed this, letting my left shoulder slump right down.

'Ttt. Looks like a broken collarbone,' Miss Hornby decided.

'It's all right, Tiffany. As soon as you feel able to stand, we'll get you to the house and call your parents. Between us, we'll decide what's best to do.'

My plan was working well so far.

They put me to bed with my arm in a sling. Then Jerry Foster, the warden guy at Frizinghall, who I've seen around the place dressed in too-short jeans, boots and a big checked shirt, took a look at me and said he didn't think the collar bone was broken.

Thanks, Jerry.

Miss Hornby frowned and said she'd already phoned Mum. 'Mrs Little is on her way to see for herself. I told her that we'd wait until she arrived before we decided whether or not to have the shoulder X-rayed.

'I don't think there'll be any need for that,' Jerry Know-All said, looking me right in the eye.

Rats!

'No, I expect you're right. In any case, even if she has broken it, there'll be so much swelling around the crack that it probably won't show up on an X-ray.'

They went away mumbling medical opinions.

Rats! I mean, really rats! I didn't mean for them to ring Mum. And Warden Jerry smells one – a rat, I mean. Now what am I gonna do?

Actually, my shoulder really does hurt. Not as much as I made out, but it definitely aches from when I fell face down on the raft.

I missed lunch.

No one came to visit.

There's a big clock on the wall with a loud tick. No telly.

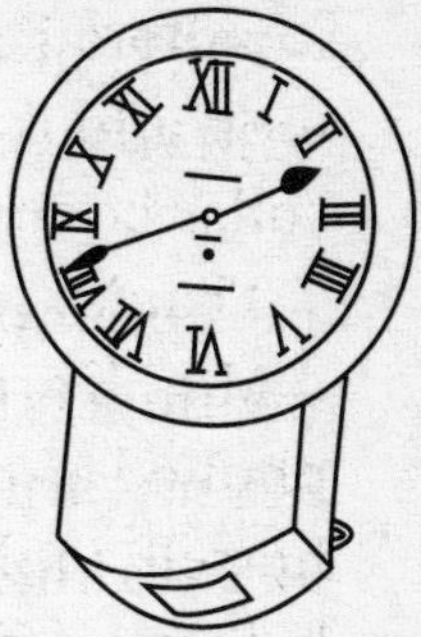

Called Mum on her mobile. She was already halfway up the motorway.

'Tiffany, where are you? Have they taken you to Casualty?'

'No, I'm still at the Hall. They're waiting until you get here before they decide about hospital.'

'But your teacher said you'd broken your collarbone. She couldn't get hold of Ross, so they phoned me at work and asked me to come up.'

I tried to sound injured but brave. 'Don't worry. It might not be broken.'

Mum was set on fearing the worst. 'Poor love. Does it hurt a lot?'

'Not too bad.'

The signal began to break up, but I managed to hear her say, 'How did it happen?'

'White water rafting.'

' . . . risky . . . safety regulations . . . teachers . . . supervise . . . dangerous . . . look into it . . .'

'Mum, you're breaking up. Can you hear me?'

'Not very well . . . twenty minutes . . . we'll soon be there.'

Click, hiss, silence.

'*We'll* soon be there'?

I tested my shoulder in secret. I can still wiggle my fingers no problem. And the truth is I can lift my arm as much as I want. Maybe I was so into the whole thing of convincing Miss H that my mind played a trick and made me think it really was hurting. Me and my mega imagination!

All I wanted was to fake a little accident and get out of rock climbing. Now look!

Mystery solved. When Mum said 'we', she meant her and Neil. Neil works for the same double glazing firm, so he was there when Mum took the phone call from Hornby. Super-boyfriend zaps in with, 'Leave it to me, Gina! I'll fix things with the boss and drive you up. I don't want you going through this alone!'

By the time Mum got here, she was in bits. She probably expected to find me covered in blood and half-drowned. Her side of the family is where I get my imagination from, I s'pose.

Neil was all calm and practical. He brought a chair to the bedside and sat Mum down.

'Tiff, how does it feel? Have they given you anything for the pain? Let me see!'

The collarbone is the thin ridge that runs from your neck to your shoulder. Mum poked it a bit, and I had to go 'ouch!' It's ages since I've been ill and had Mum fussing over me, like when I was little and had loads of ear infections. She stayed off work and I took banana flavoured medicine. It used to be weird staying at home, knowing everyone else was at school. Weird, but warm and cosy in bed with the telly on, like being inside a cocoon.

'There's no obvious bump to show that the bone is broken,' Neil said. He's the groomed type that never has a hair out of place, who looks good in a suit.

I moaned and croaked a bit more to make him shut up.

'Miss Hornby said you were concussed,' Mum went on.

I nodded woozily.

She turned to Neil. 'Shouldn't they take her to hospital just to check that out?'

'Tiff, were you actually unconscious?' he asked. As if he cared.

'Uh-uh, just dizzy.'

'Was it the back of your head, or the front?'

'Front.'

'Were you wearing a helmet?'

Another weary nod from me.

'Then I think it's OK,' Mr Medical Man told Mum. 'What I would do is put her arm in a sling and keep her in bed till tomorrow. I don't think she's come to any real harm.'

Smarmy smarty pants patted my hand and went off to find whoever was in charge.

Mum sat with me for a while. 'You had me scared back there.'

'Sorry.' I meant it. (Must never pull the fake injury stunt again. It causes too much hassle.)

Silence, wih Mum shuffling her feet and inspecting her nails. Then she came up with, 'Tiff, are you OK in general? I mean, are things all right at home with you, Scott and your dad?'

'Yeah, why shouldn't they be?' I don't want her thinking we can't manage. At the same time, the thing I want most in the world is for her to come back home. 'Bud mopes when you're not there though.'

How sad is that? She asks me how we are, and I tell her that the DOG is missing her!

Thursday, October 17th

Your stars – Get out the double-sided sticky tape, paint-brushes and pipe-cleaners – let rip with your creative streak today!

Well, I did spend half the night working on *The Voice*, my spooky moorland horror story. The ghost of the dead brother is roaming around the house at night, sending the people who live there crazy. I've jumped from the 1600s to now, with a modern family wondering where on earth the ghostly voice is coming from:

'Melanie felt a strong sensation – not a voice, nothing so definite. It was more of a beat inside her head, the throb of blood. Then a rushing sound, like the inside of a seashell. Then the cold, clammy feeling like a rising tide, as if the lake was rising to flood the house. She felt she was drowning, heard a whisper of leaves drifting through the air . . . '

Late last night Miss Westlake popped her head around the door to see how I was. 'Tough luck,' she said. 'First Chucky, now you. At this rate, we'll have the whole of Year 7 hobbling around on crutches!'

I grinned palely from my bed. Geri, Ellie and Shah were perched around the edge, in the middle of telling me about the rocks they'd climbed.

'Now that you've got spare time on your hands, how about writing us that song?' Heather breezed. 'I take it you won't be fit to do anything energetic over the next couple of days?'

'Poor you!' Geri sighed after she'd gone. 'Honestly, Tiff, I'd go nuts if I had to stay in bed while everyone is having such a cool time!'

'Uh-huh-huh.' I shifted position and gave a gentle moan.

'You should've seen us on this rockface!' Ellie jumped up and demonstrated how they'd reached for handholds and stuck their toes into tiny crevices. 'And you know how I hate heights!

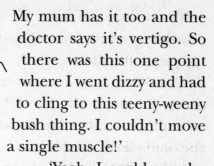

My mum has it too and the doctor says it's vertigo. So there was this one point where I went dizzy and had to cling to this teeny-weeny bush thing. I couldn't move a single muscle!'

'Yeah, I could see she was having a mega panic!' Geri jumped in. 'So I climbed up with Shah and between us we managed to talk her out of it.'

'I finally made it to the top!' Ellie bounced back on to the bed. 'And guess what, I'm cured! I'm never gonna be scared of heights ever again!'

'To change the subject, what happened with your mum?' Shah asked. 'Did she get here yet?'

'Yeah. Her boyfriend brought her.' I dropped that in to see how they would react.

'Bummer,' Geri said after a short silence.

'Yeah, bummer,' Ellie agreed. Then she leaned forward and spoke in an excited whisper. 'Anyway, what's he like?'

Shah stopped her poking her nose in any further. 'Ellie!'

'What?' She didn't get it.

'Not right now, OK? Does it look like Tiff is in the mood to talk about it?'

'It was her that mentioned it,' Ellie pointed out.

'Yeah, yeah, Mizz Caring and Sensitive!' Shah doesn't usually stand up to Ellie, but she did now. 'Listen, Tiff, d'you want anything bringing up from the kitchen? You must be starving!'

I shook my head. I hadn't got round to telling them that Mum and Neil had arranged to stay over at Frizinghall. They're sticking around to make sure I'm OK. If I'm fit to move, the plan is that they take me back to their place later today.

'Have one of these. 'Geri dug into her pocket and brought out a sticky, half eaten KitKat. 'Go on, Tiff, take it. I've got loads left, and this'll only go soggy if I keep it much longer!'

This is the last sane thing that happened before the world went mad.

It was already wild, with me faking the shoulder thing and Mum and Neil doing their Save-The-Children dash. But that was zilch compared with this morning.

Mum had got ready to give Miss Hornby an

ear-bashing for exposing her daughter to unnecessary danger, and go into her wasn't-it-a-good-thing-that-nothing-worse-had-happened rant.

Neil was standing by, looking at his watch. We were in the entrance hall, me with my mangey Adidas bag packed and ready to leave.

I was thinking, Well, the plan worked in the end, but maybe it wasn't worth it cos now I had to go and stay with Neil and Mum – bummer! – and I was actually gonna miss out on the last night party at Freezing Hole that I'd just found out about from Ellie.

'Poor you!' she cooed. 'Marc, Dom and me are gonna sing, and I'm gonna tell Heather to make Shah join in. We'll do all the numbers we've rehearsed for our first Gemini gig. Plus there'll be party food and a disco!'

Wowee! C'mon, Leo, you should be struttin' your stuff, the focus of attention, not slopping around in slippers at your mum's place!

THEN a soaking-wet Marc and Nic showed up at the main door minus Scott.

'What are you two doing

back here already?' Hornby jumped like she'd had an electric shock. 'There's another twenty-four hours before you're even due to pack your tents and leave the mountain!'

Marc staggered to a halt outside the door, letting Nic come in and drip all over the stone floor. Nic was white as a sheet.

'Don't tell me you chickened out of the challenge just because of a spot of rain!' our kind and loving group tutor accused him.

Nic shook his head, spraying water over me. He drew a deep breath. 'Scott got lost!' he gasped.

'Who? . . . How? . . . What d'you mean, "Scott got lost"?'

Miss Hornby wasn't the only one who couldn't take it in. I saw Mum frown, pick up my bag, think again and put it down in a puddle. Neil's face flickered from a frown to a grin, like – *Oh yeah, very funny, ha-ha!*

'I'm serious!' Nic insisted. 'We were up on Pike's Needle, camping by a stream. It was the middle of the night when Scott decided he needed to go outside for a pee. Me and Marc didn't take much notice, just sort of turned over and went back to sleep. But when we woke up

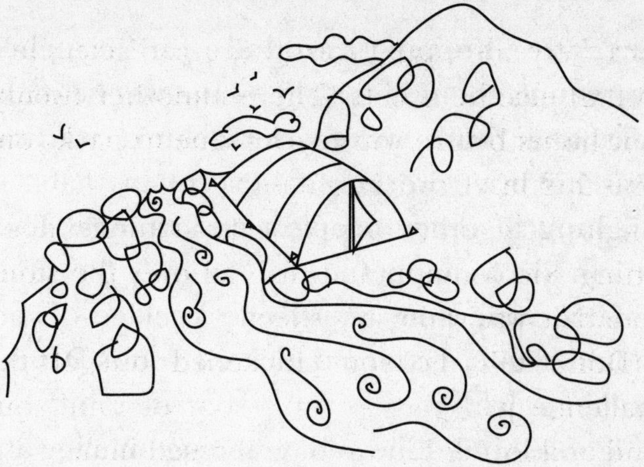

this morning, Scott's sleeping bag was still empty. It looks like he just never came back!'

'I don't believe it!'

'It's a scam!'

'Trust Scott Little!'

I could go on and on with the sort of comments that came back when the news got out.

While Mum flapped, Neil frowned and Hornby went ballistic with Nic and Marc for leaving my brother alone on the mountain, Chucky Gilbert limped up and insulted my family.

'You Littles are a disaster zone!' he cawed.

This is a kid who fell downstairs and is

currently hopping around on crutches! Everything about him is slow – the way he walks, talks and thinks (clunk-clunk-clunk, you can hear his brain working) – except his habit of laughing at other people's misfortunes. Then he's in like a whippet.

'First you, now Scott!' he cackled. 'They should stick a Hazard notice on you – Danger. Do not touch!'

'Ignore him!' Ellie said, grabbing my sling and whisking me away into the Games Room.

'Ooch-ooch, ouch!' I reminded her. (The show must go on!)

Geri and Shah followed us.

'Listen, Tiff,' Ellie said, giving me a quick hug.

'Ooch-ouch!'

'We're really gutted for you. Is there anything we can do?'

'We could form a search party and go looking for Scott!' Action Girl Geri suggested. 'I mean it. It might be ages before the Mountain Rescue team gets itself together. We could be halfway up Pike's Needle before they even leave their base.'

Chucky's words were still ringing in my ears. And I couldn't get Mum's gob-smacked face out of my mind. I had to dash and find her. 'Ask permission before you go,' I muttered before hurrying off.

Mum and Neil were still in the entrance hall with Hornby, Nic and Marc. A big crowd of kids had gathered, together with Heather, George and Jerry Foster. So everything was pretty chaotic.

'Let me get this straight.' The warden had practically pinned Nic and Marc against the wall. 'Scott has been out in the open for most of the night. It's been raining non-stop, the temperature fell to 2 degrees. As far as you know, he didn't have any waterproof clothing on?'

Nic shook his head. 'His boots and fleece were missing from the tent though, so we reckon he must've been wearing those.'

'When he went out for a pee?' Jerry scratched his head. 'How can a fifteen-year-old kid get lost by popping outside to relieve his bladder?'

Chucky, Squealer and a crowd of other boys sniggered.

'Cut it out!' Mr Fox told them.

But to tell the truth, I was on Jerry Foster's wave-length. I mean, how could even Scott (who is no superbrain, but there again isn't completely thick) possibly get into this mess? Like, doh!

'Could he be making his way down from the mountain alone?' Heather asked. 'I mean, if Scott has any sense, he wouldn't blunder around blindly in the dark, he would wait until it was light, then come down.'

I sighed. My brother doesn't have any sense, that's the point.

Things Scott is good at:
skiving
watching telly
computer games
. . . that's it!

I could picture him blundering in the dark, no problem!

(Tiffany Little, you should show more sympathy. You are not, repeat NOT a nice person!)

Jerry Foster thought Heather had a point. 'I agree there's no need to panic just yet.'

Poor Mum jumped in with, 'What d'you mean, not panic! My boy's lost up a mountain in terrible weather and the only idea you've had so far is for us to wait for him to find his own way down!'

'Take it easy, Gina.' Neil moved in with a comforting arm around her shoulder. 'I'm sure Jerry has a routine worked out for just such a situation.'

We all turned to stare at Jerry.

The warden wrinkled his eyes then dished out the orders. 'Miss Hornby, you stay here and supervise the other students. Cancel all morning activities. Miss Westlake and Mr Fox, you both have qualifications in First Aid and Orienteering?' He waited for Heather and George to answer.

'Yeah, they were practising the kiss of life and finding their way around in the dark all last night!' Squealer whispered without moving his lips.

Chucky, Dom and Callum nearly wet themselves.

'Good. Well, you two should set out right now on the fixed route that we know the boys took up the mountain. The chances are high that you'll meet a very wet and sorry-for-himself student making his way down. Meanwhile, I'll contact the Rescue team and get them to send out three or four guys in a Land-Rover.'

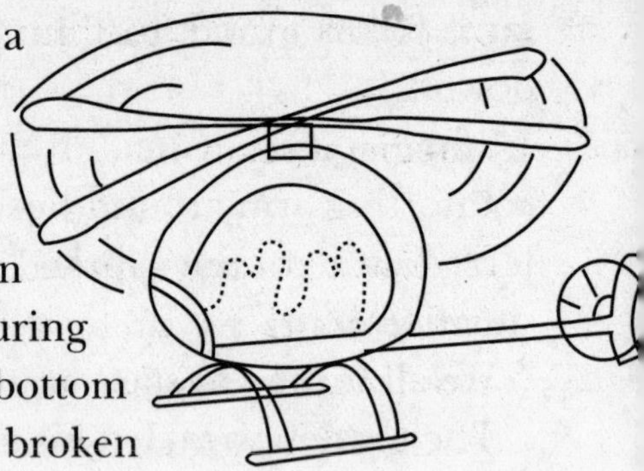

'Never mind a Land-Rover, get a helicopter!' Mum cried. The panic had really taken hold. She was picturing Scott lying in the bottom of a ravine with broken bones, at least.

So while Jerry got things moving, she pulled out her mobile.

'Who are you calling?' I asked.

'Your father. I should let him know what's happened, then he can decide for himself whether or not he wants to come up.'

I swallowed hard and glanced at Neil.

Neil nodded wisely. Good idea. But there was a little flicker behind his eyes that said, *Hang on a moment. D'you really think that Ross coming here is a good idea?*

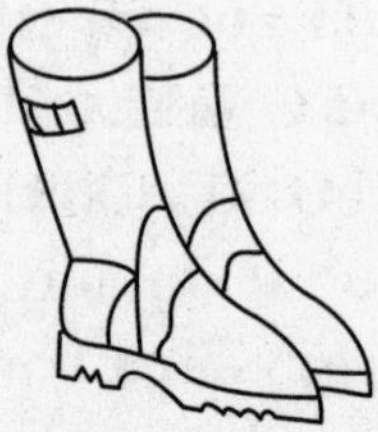

p.m. When Scott Got Lost, Part 2

It's tragic, it really is.

* What did Geri, Shah and Ellie do? They set out to search for Scott without telling anyone, even though I told them not to. THIS IS NOT A JOKE! I MEAN IT. That's what they went and did. Now no one knows where they are either. They're up a mountain somewhere, probably wandering around in circles.
* Dad arrived just before lunch.
* Scott is still missing.

Here's how the newspaper headline will look:

MOUNTAIN CLAIMS FOUR YOUNG LIVES!

BRAVE THREESOME DIE IN FAILED ATTEMPT TO RESCUE INJURED SCHOOL CHUM!!!

School photos of Scott, Geri, Shah and Ellie will stare out of TV screens all over the country. Safety standards at Frizinghall will come under scrutiny. There will be interviews with bereaved relatives.

MINISTER CALLS FOR NATIONWIDE REVIEW OF SCHOOL TRIPS!

STORM BREWS OVER OUTDOOR PURSUITS!

TRAGIC FAMILIES BUILD MEMORIAL ON MOUNTAIN!

Journalists will crawl all over our private lives.

WAS TRAGIC SCHOOLBOY'S DEATH SUICIDE?

Exclusive report.

NewsTeam reporter, Gavin Steele, has uncovered a possible motive for 15 year old Scott Little's fatal fall from Pike's Needle in October this year. Detailed investigation has uncovered deep unhappiness in the Ashbrook pupil's family circumstances. Parents Ross (38) and Gina (36) had recently split, leaving Scott and his sister, Tiffany (11) in the care of their father.

Scott had spoken to friends of his distress. One, Marc Ainsworth (15), is quoted as saying, 'No way did Scott want his mum to leave home. From being a normal, laid back mate, he turned into a moody loner who stuck himself in front of a computer screen 24/7. You couldn't talk to him. He just wasn't the same Scott Little any more.'

Police involved in the investigation into the deaths have not ruled out a possible suicide. 'Taking into consideration the position of the body and the unusual circumstances behind Scott's disappearance from the tent, we certainly haven't ruled it out,' a spokesperson told us earlier today.

However, the police have closed their files on the deaths by drowning of 11-year-old Ellie Shelbourn and Fuchsia Allerton, plus twelve-year-old Geri Shapiro. The three close friends apparently died in a vain effort to reach Scott's body, which lay in a ravine at the far side of a little known mountain lake. 'It was a heroic rescue attempt that went tragically wrong,' the spokesman concluded. 'Our sympathy goes out to all the families.'

This could happen!!! It may be a little far-fetched, I admit. But it definitely could turn out this way!

Career Note: Stick with creative writing and steer clear of journalism. I couldn't stand poking around for news and making people feel bad. 'Hello, Mrs Smith. I'm from The Daily Mars. Your husband/son/father has just been arrested for kidnapping the Prime Minister. Could you give us your reaction please?'

There again, knowing Scott, maybe it'll turn out to be not so tragic after all.

I just overheard Marc telling some kids from my year that he reckoned Scott had chickened out of spending any more nights on the mountain. Marc's theory was that my precious bro had deliberately taken off with a torch and a compass. 'Scott's not stupid. He probably found the nearest road and hitch-hiked back home to see the next episode of Corrie.'

Lisa Sharman and Callum went, 'Wow!' and 'How come?'

'Because, like I said, Scott's not thick. It was Nic who lost it when we woke up and found the empty sleeping bag. I said not to worry, Scott could look after himself, and anyhow he probably didn't want to be found. But Nic kept saying Scott wouldn't do that, not without telling us. I said, don't you believe it. In the end, I said OK, let's go and tell Hornby, mainly because I'm not thick either and I wanted to get out of the rain. Reporting Scott missing was the best way of doing it!'

The new rumour spread through the Hall like wildfire.

'You mean, we're stuck in here doin' nothin' because Scott Little nicked off?'

'Typical!'

'Wouldn't you just know it, the selfish gi . . .!'

'Dominic!' Hornby pounced. 'Please go and tell Mrs Little that Mr Little has just arrived.'

I took a deep breath then stepped outside to meet Dad.

He'd rattled all the way up the motorway in his beaten up white van with bits of orange string holding the back doors closed. He was in his paint splattered work jeans, opening the passenger door and letting Bud jump out and start sniffing around.

He saw me. 'Tiff, what's going on? Has Scott shown up yet?'

I shook my head.

He noticed my arm in a sling. 'What happened?'

I went hot under the collarbone! 'I had an accident. The school tried to ring you. Mum's here with . . .'

'Yeah, yeah, I know all that. But your mum's message was pretty garbled. I couldn't make much sense of what she was telling me.' Dad's mind flitted around, trying to take in the big old, spooky hall, the rain blasting across the misty fells and the dozens of curious faces gawping at him through the windows. 'Has Scott really gone missing, or is it your mum doing her usual hysterical, over-the-top routine?'

It was the first time I'd EVER heard Dad say something nasty about Mum. Through everything – the separation, the rows about money, he'd never once badmouthed her to me or Scott.

Now, should I answer with a straight 'yes', or should Nasty, Not Nice Me tell him that maybe Scott had faked the whole thing? I was stammering and stuttering when Mum flew out into the yard.

'Ross, you made it! It's OK, everything's in hand. The warden has contacted the Mountain Rescue team. Two teachers have already gone out looking. They're doing all they possibly can to find Scott and bring him back down before nightfall!'

I saw Dad's face go deadly serious. So this was the real thing, not just one of Mum's nervous breakdowns. 'What do they think happened?'

Mum gave him the facts. 'We were already up here, looking after Tiff . . .'

'"We"?' Dad echoed.

Oh no, he didn't know the bit about Neil being here! I wanted to whisk him away, beam him up to another planet to spare him the next moment.

Mum hesitated. When Bud spied her and

lolloped up, she pushed him away. 'Me and Neil,' she whispered.

We all turned to see the man-in-the-suit himself walking towards us with an umbrella.

'Oh yeah, right!' Dad mumbled. He couldn't even be bothered to fake a polite hello. He just grabbed hold of Bud's collar and stood there, looking lost, with rain streaming down his face.

A bit later, we sat in the dining room, studying a map of the area.

Jerry Foster had spread it out on the table and marked certain spots with red felt-tip.

'Here's the Hall,' he pointed out.

I remembered Neil's brolly turning inside-out in the wind, and Dad's face going stiff and blank.

'And here's Pike's Needle, where the three boys made camp.'

I could see Dad now, studying the map with a pained expression. Bud sat under his chair, tongue lolling on to the stone flags.

'What's this?' Mum pointed to a blue blob on the map.

'That's Pike's Tarn, a small lake to the north of the Three Cols.'

Oh no! The nightmare newspaper headline came back to haunt me –

BRAVE THREESOME DIE . . .

'Is anyone out looking for Shah, Geri and Ellie?' I demanded in a shaky voice.

The fact that my three best mates had snuck off on their own rescue attempt hadn't attracted much notice so far.

'I've notified the Mountain Rescue team,' Jerry insisted. 'They're not too concerned about the girls right now. As long as they stick together and keep their heads, they'll be OK.'

Dad frowned. 'I'm not happy with that.' Looking out of the long window at the drenching rain, he made a snap decision. 'C'mon, Bud!' he said, scraping his chair back and standing up.

'Oh Ross, sit down and listen!' Mum sighed.

'You mean, twiddle my thumbs while Scott and the girls get themselves more and more lost!'

Dad wasn't having any of it. He strode towards the door with Bud plodding behind.

Neil got up to follow them. 'Maybe it wouldn't be such a good idea . . .'

Dad turned and dead eyed him. 'It's *my* son we're talking about,' he said quietly.

Which put Neil in his place.

'Dad, wait for me!' I hared after him and Bud.

'Tiffany, come back! You've hurt your shoulder, you're . . .'

'Let me come,' I pleaded with Dad. It was my brother and my friends they were talking about!

'You think you can manage?' he asked.

I nodded. 'Wait a sec, I'll grab a couple of cagoules from the cloakroom.'

And that was how come, give or take a shriek and groan from Mum, that Dad, Bud and me were out on the fells in the mist and rain.

p.m. When Scott Got Lost, Part 3

Honestly, you watch vids and read books, but you never think you'll be doing the Bruce Willis stuff yourself. I mean, this was for real!

What's the use of a poxy cagoule that's not

waterproof? Dad and me were soaked to the skin before we'd even battled our way against the wind through the tall stone gateposts of Frizinghall.

'Ross Little, I'll never forgive you if anything happens to Tiffany!' Mum's last words rung in my ears.

Neil was the one who persuaded her to let me go, I'll give him that. He'd shoved a map into the kangaroo pocket of my cagoule, along with his mobile phone. 'We'll let you know if we hear any news,' he promised. 'And don't stay out too long. It'll get dark pretty early tonight, what with all this cloud hanging around.'

So we had useless cagoules, a map, a phone and Bud. There were miles of empty mountains, caves, cliffs, heather and lakes ahead of us, black clouds overhead and rain coming down in buckets.

No one in their right minds would be out – only Miss Westlake, Mr Fox, us, Shah, Geri, Ellie and of course Scott! Plus an official Mountain Rescue Land-Rover tearing across the moors from their control centre in town.

As we sploshed through puddles and took a track away from Frizinghall Lake, I thought I'd better come clean with Dad.

'There's this rumour,' I began. It was hard to find the exact words to explain.

'What rumour?' Dad strode ahead, watching Bud sniff around in the heather.

'About Scott. Umm – They're saying – I'm not sure if it's actually true – er – he might've deliberately on purpose got himself lost.' Yeah, well done, Tiff. Very well put. Nice one!

Dad stopped dead.

Bud sniffed a bit more then shot off through the bushes.

'Why would Scott do that?' Dad asked slowly. 'No, don't tell me, he's skived off home without telling anyone!'

I shrugged. 'That's what they're kind of saying.'

'Oh great!' Dad peered up ahead at the lashing rain. 'If it's true, I'll kill 'im with my bare hands!'

Note for The Voice: 'Rain sweeps down the hillside, wave after wave, driven by the wind. Black thorn trees bend under it, the sheep take shelter . . . purple clouds swirling . . . deserted horizon . . . '

Dad turned to me. 'What d'you think, Tiff?'

Raindrops trickled off the end of my nose. 'Dunno.' I thought a while, then went into major cofession mode. 'I reckon Scott would hate every second he spent in that tent once it started to rain, and knowing him he'd be thinking of a way out.'

'But he's supposed to be in training for Patagonia!' Dad was way too nice to understand Scott's devious mind.

I watched Bud circle around and turn back towards us. He was barking like crazy all the way down the hill. 'Yeah, but he could invent a reason to skive, couldn't he?'

'Like what?'

'Like an injury for instance.'

Note 2 – 'Cold rain trickled down the back of Melanie's neck. It felt like icy fingers probing her spine, sending shivers through her whole body. Somewhere out there in the storm, the owner of the ghostly voice waited . . . "Vengeance!" it whispered. "I will have revenge for my most foul murder!"'

'Scott wouldn't do that!' Dad said as Bud blundered through the bushes.

I had to convince him, so I fiddled under my cagoule and untied my sling. I held my arm up and wiggled my fingers. '*I* did!' I whispered. 'And honest, Dad, Scott's twice as bad as me!'

Luckily, Bud's barking took Dad's mind off the awful truth about his kids.

Now, no way is Bud a smart, alert German shepherd, police-tracker-and-sniffer type of dog. Lazy slob is more his style. He only usually moves when food is stuck under his nose, or when next door's thick cat wanders into our garden. So to see him bouncing up at Dad and barking was a one-off.

'Get down!' Dad grabbed his muddy paws and made him sit.

'Tiff,' he said with a catch in his voice, 'I just don't know what to think . . .'

'Woof!' (*Look, you idiot!*)

'I'm sorry, Dad. But white water rafting and rock climbing isn't my thing!'

'Woof-woof, Grrrruff!' (*Can't you understand what I'm trying to tell you!*)

'Down, Bud! You're saying Scott is capable of doing what you did, only worse!'

Poor Dad. The idea of Mountain Rescue coming out on a wild goose chase was more than he could bear. Did I feel guilty!

Guilt = a churning in your stomach and a clammy feeling in the palms of your hands. An 'Oh no!' groan goes right through your body. You know the word sorry isn't enough.

'I don't know for sure that Scott is skiving,' I muttered. 'It might be genuine for all I know.'

'Woof-*beeping*-woof!' Bud grabbed the hem of Dad's cagoule and tugged him up the hill.

He made us look up at last, and who did we see emerging through the mist and rain? . . .. Da-da-dah . . .!

(Always end a chapter/section/paragraph on a cliff-hanging moment. This is Gorgeous George's advice whenever we start a story-writing project.)

. . . First I made out Ellie in her bright orange Goretex. She was waving like mad to attract our attention.

'Woof . . .grrr!' (*About blooming time!*)

Then, four more figures materialized – Shah, Geri, Heather and George. But no Scott. My heart bump-bump-bumped, then thudded. Like when you skim a pebble on water – skim-skim-skim-splash! They staggered and splashed their way down while we squelched up.

'Is there any news?' Dad yelled.

I prayed for them to say yes, Scott was lagging behind but he was fine.

'Mr Little!' The wind blew Ellie bang into him. 'We're sorry, we really are!'

Which didn't give us any facts to go on, but sure scared the pants off us.

I saw Scott lying dead in a pool of blood at the foot of a cliff. His body was stiff and cold . . .

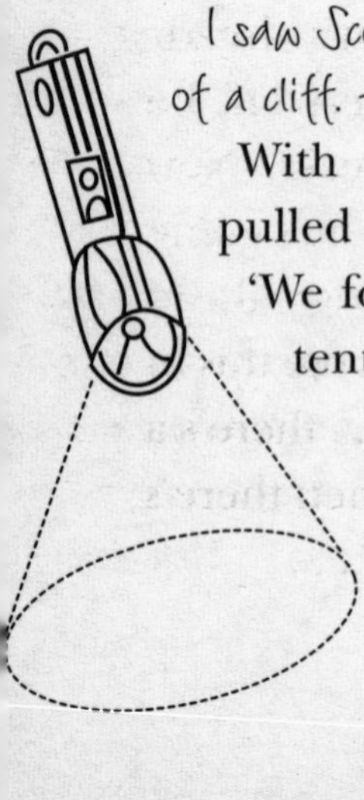

With a great sense of timing, Ellie slowly pulled a torch out of her (bone-dry) pocket.

'We found it two hundred metres from the tent,' she said gravely.

'It must belong to Scott,' Geri explained. 'It means he dropped it in the dark and lost his way.'

'Then George and I came along and found the girls.' Heather took over. 'We called the Hall and discovered they didn't have permission to be out here, so we're having to take them back before we can carry on with the search.'

'Yeah, but we found the only bit of evidence so far,' Ellie argued. 'I don't see why we're in trouble.'

This was the first time I ever saw George get heavy and talk like a teacher. 'You're in trouble, young lady, because you tried something extremely foolhardy and dangerous. You've no idea how treacherous these fells can be. You're lucky you didn't end up with a broken ankle or something much worse!'

Ellie sniffed. 'We were only trying to help.'

Meanwhile, I was getting to grips with the torch situation. This is the scene – Scott gets up to go for a pee. He grabs a torch, or maybe it's already in his pocket. He goes out and wanders off, he stumbles, drops the torch, which breaks. Now he's totally lost. He staggers on, hoping he's going back the way he came. But there's a ledge ahead and it leads to a sheer drop. Scott can't see this in the dark. His foot slips over the edge . . . there's a scream. His body hits the ground . . . then there's the blood bit and the cold, stiff corpse . . .

I could see that this was also the way Dad was thinking. 'You take the girls back to the Hall,' he told Heather and George. 'Tiffany and I will go ahead.'

'You're sure you can find the way?' George asked. 'It's pretty dangerous up there if you don't know the territory.'

I tapped my kangaroo pouch to show that we had a map.

'Let me go back with them!' Geri pleaded. 'It'd be much quicker!'

Heather was shaking her head when Dad interrupted. 'That's OK, I'll take charge of her. It'll be my responsibility if anything happens.'

Reluctantly Heather and George agreed. I noticed we didn't get any argument from Ellie and Shah. Shah was like a drowned rat, poor thing, and Ellie was probably worried about catching a cold and losing her voice.

'Good luck!' Shah whispered, as Bud charged off up the hill again.

I tell you, life's not fair. Shah has a new half-sister who she dreads meeting. I have a brother who gives us nothing but hassle. Right now I wouldn't care if I never saw him ever again! Where's the justice in that?

So I smiled at her and told her not to worry, Scott was tough as old boots and I'd see her later. Then I drew her to one side. 'When you get back to the Hall, can you do me a favour?' Shah nodded.

'I just remembered, I left my diary on my pillow and forgot to lock it. The key's in the top drawer of my locker. D'you think you could . . .?'

'Sure, no problem.' Shah smiled. I trusted her and she knew that I did.

No need even for her to say, 'Don't worry, I won't read it.' Unlike with Ellie, who's definitely not that reliable. It sounds horrible, but you're never quite sure whether Ellie's gonna turn around and stab you in the back.

'C'mon, Tiff!' Geri yelled from a hundred metres up the hill. You'd never have thought she'd been up and down the mountain once already.

So I cut the chat and sprinted (a sprint that turns into a squelch is probably a sprelch.) Splosh-splosh-trip-sprelch!

'How far before we reach the tents?' Dad gasped. He was fit, but not as fit as Geri.

'About twenty minutes if we run all the way.'

After ten, even Bud was tiring. Either that, or he'd smelt something interesting. 'Look at the dog!' I told Dad.

'Not now, Tiff!' His chest was heaving in and out and his legs looked weary.

Geri, on the other hand, was springing through the heather like a young lamb – hop-skippety-hop!

'No, Dad, look!' Bud had sniffed-trotted-sniffed-and-loped at a diagonal across the hillside, looking something like a proper tracker dog at work for once. Nose to the ground, tail up and super-eager.

Dad glanced towards the horizon to our right. 'What's he up to?'

I stopped to draw breath. 'Maybe he's on to something.' There again, did Bud have the brainpower to suss out that Scott was lost and that we were up here looking for him?

'Nah!' Dad shook his head, intending to

follow Geri all the way to the tents.

'Nah!' I agreed.

Until Bud went into his woof-woofing routine, meaning *hey, you stupid humans, why don't you listen to me!*

'Dad, I think we'd better take a look!' I called. But he and Geri must've been too far ahead, because they took no notice.

OK, so it was up to me to drag Bud back on course. I stomped across to where the stupid mutt teetered on the edge of a ledge.

Aaagh! The ledge looked down on to a sheer cliff. I went dizzy, just like Ellie. Vertigo! 'Come back, Bud!' I pleaded. The dog was staring down a ten metre drop, whining and crouching with his ears laid back.

'I mean it, Bud. Stop messing around!' I couldn't even bear to look, so I grabbed his collar and tugged.

The thing is, I just couldn't picture Bud doing anything smart. I mean, normally he has the attention span of a gnat. Having him suddenly turn into Super-Sleuth was too much to take in. Anyhow, dogs aren't heroes in real life.

This is just to prepare for the fact that this is exactly what Budweiser, our tatty, overweight

German shepherd did (which I know takes away the suspense and therefore breaks every rule in the creative writing book. But what the heck?)

'Woof!' A sharp bark pierced the silence of the ravine.

'Woof!' The faint echo came back muffled by the wind and rain.

Bud pulled himself free of my grasp and sought out a zig-zag track which led down the steep slope. The path was overgrown with ferns and brambles, but Bud barrelled on and I followed, grabbing at bushes for handholds and feeling my wellies slide through the mud. We splashed through a stream, where I plunged knee deep in icy water, fell forward and sat up to my waist, while my dog shook himself on the far bank. I nearly died of hypo-whatsit there and then.

'Woof-woof!' Bud encouraged. He reached a twisted hawthorn tree growing out of a gap in the rock, where he whined and scrabbled at the base of the trunk.

'OK, OK, I'm coming!' Slip-slop-drip!

'Whoof-whine-whinge!' Scrabble-scrabble.

I fought through brambles, ooch-ouch!, and joined Bud by the tree.

Scott lay on his side with his back to me, his front half draped across a fallen branch, one leg folded awkwardly under him. Rain spattered down from the tree on to his sodden cagoule.

I felt my heart thump then miss a beat, jumped the log and fell on my knees beside him. His eyes were closed. Wildly I wondered what to do. Don't move him to begin with, lean right down to listen to his breathing; if no pulse, prepare to give the kiss of life.

I heaved Scott on to his back and unzipped his cagoule.

His brown eyes opened and he stared at me. 'Gotcha!' he croaked.

Ha-ha! – NOT! I nearly went nuts. He's lucky I didn't strangle him.

'Hey, back off!' he yelled when I tried to jerk

him on to his stupid feet. 'I've got a broken ankle here!'

'Yeah, yeah!' I pulled and yanked.

'I mean it. Why d'you think I'm out here in the *beeping* rain, waiting for you lot to *beeping* find me?'

There's gratitude for you. Bud and I save Scott's life and all he does is swear!

'Couldn't you have tried hopping back to the Hall?' I demanded. 'You've still got one good ankle, haven't you!'

'Yeah well, that's what I was doin' in the dark before I overbalanced and fell down this *beep-beeping* ravine,' he huffed. 'You certainly took your time to come and find me – I'm *beeping* starving!'

Well, if he was gonna be like that, I wasn't gonna waste any sympathy. Instead, I unzipped my pocket and reached for the mobile. Uh-oh! It was totally, one hundred per cent dripping wet inside the kangaroo pouch. The pocket had collected half a litre of water during my swim in the stream, so I had no chance of getting it to work. 'Bud, sit!' I growled at our dog-hero.

Bud was already sitting, so he flopped down beside Scott.

'That's a good dog, stay here!'

'Hey, where are you goin'?' Scott panicked. 'You can't leave me! Tiffany, come back!'

That was how it feels to have power. A kind of secret gloating glow in my stomach. Nasty Me said, 'Go on, let him think you're scarpering. Leave him in the dark!' But Not-So-Nasty Me owed him an explanation.

'It's OK, don't go into a strop. I'm only running to fetch Dad and Geri. I'll be back in ten minutes, you just wait here!'

'*Beep-beeping beep*!' I heard as I scrambled out of the ravine. Scott's voice merged into the hiss of the rain. 'With this busted ankle I'm not going any-*beeping*-where!'

Saturday, October 19th

Your stars – Leos would rather act in a play than watch one. So design a drama with a bunch of mates and make sure you're the star of the show!

Life's way too dramatic already. This week just about gave me a heart attack, thank you very much!

So Scott got lost for real, and the broken ankle was genuine too. But that's not all.

Mountain Rescue finally made it and zoomed him off to hospital. Mum made a big fuss of Bud and promised to bring him a treat when he got back home.

Oh, and Shah, Geri, Ellie and me all got banned from Frizinghall and sent back home. That was yesterday, after everything had calmed down.

Reasons:

Me for faking the broken collarbone (Dad dobbed me in)

Geri, Ellie and Shah for breaking every rule in the outdoor pursuits book.

Geri's really down about it. Her pursuits have been cut off in their prime. Ellie sulked because she missed the Friday party. Shah got it in the neck from her dad, who's been getting it in the neck all week himself from her mum. 'I never thought I'd see the day when any daughter of mine . . .'

She only tried to help find Scott, for God's sake!

Ellie's mum and dad are on her side, natch. They promised they'd take it up with school on Monday. Mr Shelbourn must be the parent from hell as far as the teachers go. He's the type who's always in the right, Mr Big, Successful Architect.

Meanwhile, Mrs S says Ellie can have a sleepover tonight.

I wore Dad down until in the end he agreed I could go.

Items to pack:
- jim-jams
- knickers
- toothbrush
- make-up
- hairbrush

Make-up is stashed under bed in wussy pencil case given to me by Gran Jackson at the start of term. Would rather die than take said case with shiny purple dinosaurs into school. But it's useful for the eyeliners and lippies that Dad won't let me wear (humph!).

Scott is stomping around the house like a

pirate. His leg's in a pot up to the knee. He keeps waving his crutch and saying 'Avast mi hairies!' to anyone who'll listen. (He means 'hearties', but Scott likes to be different.) He made a silver medal for Bud out of chocolate foil and parcel ribbon, then pinned it to his collar. I swear the mutt is going round the house smirking!

Mum dropped in just after lunch. No doggy treats though.

I could tell from her face that SOMETHING WAS WRONG!

Dad answered the door. I was standing at the top of the stairs wih my bag packed ready for tonight. Scott had his pot leg up in front of the telly.

There was this long pause, then Mum said, 'Can I come in?' Dad stood to one side and Mum squeezed past.

Normally Mum looks cool. She's young for her age and goes to the gym etc. But today she looked BAD – puffy red eyes, smudged mouth, greasy hair.

'Scott, your mother's here!' Dad yelled into the living-room. 'I presume that's who you came to see?' he said to Mum in this prim, un-Dadlike voice. The he went out of the front door, jumped into his van and drove off.

Mum glanced up at me and I guessed – she'd had a row with Neil. She didn't have to tell me in words, I just knew.

She met my eyes. 'Neil walked out,' she sighed. Her shoulders slumped and she curled forward as if someone had punched her in the stomach. But then she made an effort to pull herself together – shoulders back, chin up. 'Well, that's up to him, isn't it? I'm not gonna lose any sleep wondering whether or not he'll cool down and come creeping back!'

I kind of grimaced and backed off into my room. I mean, what d'you say? 'Hurrah! You broke up with Neil, now you can come back home!' or, 'Poor thing, you must be really upset. Would you like a cup of tea?' or 'Don't worry, Mum, it'll soon blow over. Your smarmy boyfriend will be back.'

Everything considered, I thought silence was the best.

Mum followed me up the stairs. 'Don't you want to know what it was about?'

'Nope.' Zzzzzippp! I checked inside my bag to make sure I'd got everything. But now that Dad had made his quick exit I'd lost my lift. 'Can you drive me over to Ellie's house?' I asked.

For a second Mum was thrown. 'What? No, I don't want anyone to see me with my face looking like this.'

Us seeing her didn't count, I suppose.

This wasn't going well, and we both knew it.

'Look, Tiff . . .'

'Sorry, Mum, I don't . . .'

We began and stopped at the same time.

'I know. My stuff with Neil is down to me,' she blubbed. 'I shouldn't be dumping it on you.'

I wanted to hug her, but didn't. 'I gotta ring Ellie and tell her I'll be late,' I muttered, while she trailed off downstairs to cheer up the invalid.

Sunday, October 20th

Your stars – *Sure, you're bold and brave, but with your Mars ruler backsliding in the sky, your sense of where you're going hasn't been strong lately. Blah-de-blah . . .*

(Dad's posh paper. Mars this, Venus that. I give up!)

This is the song we finally wrote last night for Ellie's band:

ANGEL ON THE SIDEWALK

Here she comes, she's all dressed up
She don't even notice me
Here she comes, they say she's crazy
She means all the world to me

Oh Angel on the sidewalk
Angel on the street
Oh Angel on the sidewalk
Angel Angel Angel on the street

Lights are low, she's all lit up
Coffee cups and diamond rings
Lights are low, they make her shine
Lipstick stain and angel wings

Oh Angel on the sidewalk . . .

Shah wrote the music. There's gonna be more verses. It doesn't look much on paper, but when

Ellie sings it in a husky American voice, it sounds well cool.

That took two whole hours, but it was worth it.

Then we got to talking about the two Fs – Families and Freezing Hole.

We were all sitting on Ellie's bed, sticking shiny stars on top of our blue nail varnish. Suddenly my hand started to shake and tears leaked out of my eyes. I didn't mean it to happen.

'Families!' Ellie snorted when they'd heard about Mum and Neil. 'Jeez, it's a wonder any of us turn out normal!'

Geri said her family was fine, thank you very much.

And we said she was lucky.

Ellie wished she had a brother.

'No you don't!' I tried to convince her. 'Think Scott! You definitely do NOT want a brother!'

'Yeah, but he could be like Nic Heron,' Ellie pointed out, and floated off into a little dream.

Which is when Shah chipped in with the story of her half-sister. She told it in a rush, like she had to get it out into the open.

Silence. Geri and even Motor-Mouth Ellie were gobsmacked.

'She's coming down for Christmas,' Shah told us. 'Mum's being really good about it now she's thought it through. I mean, it happened before she even knew Dad, and it's only the fact that he never mentioned it that upsets her. And it's definitely not Skye's fault.'

'Yeah, but Christmas!' Geri sighed. 'Bummer!'

'How d'you feel about it?' I asked.

Shah frowned. 'Numb. Nothing. I don't feel anything.'

These days you can lose mothers and find half-sisters at the drop of a hat. You might as well throw us all into a big lottery draw and pick out numbers – Congratulations, you belong to family number 1,567,348!

Then we got on to Freezing Hole.

'We're in deep doo-doo!' Geri said. (She watches too many American cartoons). 'Hornby and the rest are gonna kill us!'

'Yeah, we're dead!' Shah groaned.

'Can they expel us for what we did?' I wondered.

'Oh God, you're all such wusses!' Ellie scoffed. 'By the time Dad's finished with them, they'll be begging us to stay!' She flashed her fingernails at us, then pounced on me. 'Hey, and I need to have a word with you, Tiffany Little!'

'Why? What did I do?' She'd turfed me off the bed and mussed my hair. I was shedding glitter stars all over the posh carpet.

'You lied to us!' Ellie was on the warpath, pillow above her head.

'When? How?' Suddenly my voice was a hamster squeak. Shah and Geri were ganging up, grabbing pillows and advancing too.

'Yeah, you faked your collar-bone without telling us!' Geri said. In her hands, a feather pillow could turn into a lethal weapon.

'Listen, I would've told you when I got the chance!' I was backed into a corner, defenceless.

'But you cheated!' Ellie shrieked.

Huh! Mizz Number One Sneak Ellie Shelbourn was calling me a cheat! Nice one! 'What about your audition for Gemini?' I squealed.

But I got pummelled by pillows, coshed by cushions, festooned in feathers anyway.

Geri's pillow burst, wouldn't you just know!

Yeah, and a pillow fight is a bit of an anti-climax after Scott getting lost.

But hey, that's the kind of week it's been.

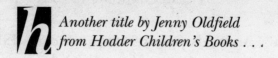

Another title by Jenny Oldfield
from Hodder Children's Books . . .

Definitely Daisy 1
You're a disgrace, Daisy!

Meet Daisy Morelli - a magnet
for trouble and a master plotter.
Whne things go wrong - and they
always do - who gets the blame?
Definitely Daisy!

Daisy's fed up with school, so
she plans to run away – chucking
in boring lessons for footballing
stardom! If only the junior
Soccer Academy will have her . . .